KU-675-882

Leo
Takes to the Stage

Zuza Vrbova

Illustrated by Tom Morgan-Jones

CHRYSALIS CHILDREN'S BOOKS

Leo had a big dressing-up box in his room.

It was full of different kinds of outfits –

and Leo loved dressing up in them.

4

When his friends came round, they made up stories
and acted them out. Leo was a very good actor –
he could make his friends laugh when he was
being funny, and cry when he was being serious.

Leo's friends loved watching him perform,
and they knew he wanted to be a famous actor
when he grew up.

Leo liked pretending to be all kinds of people, but most of all, he liked pretending to be a rock star.

One day, he decided to have a rock concert.

He learnt lots of new songs and spent ages practising.

Then he invited his friends round to watch. He jumped up and down on the bed, singing really loudly.

"Great!" shouted Tabby, jumping onto the bed too.

Then everyone jumped onto the bed, and they danced and danced. Bertie whistled loudly and Rudy hopped about happily. Even Crispin admitted it was a great rock concert.

One day, Leo was thinking about the school play.

He really wanted to get the lead role of Robin Hood.

So he decided to cut his hair specially for the part.

He made a few snips and then looked in the mirror.

Hmmm, the style is not quite right yet, Leo thought.

So he made some more snips in his hair. But the more he snipped, the worse it got. His hair got shorter and shorter.

"Oh no!" cried Leo. "There's not much hair left now!"

9

Connie, Tabby and Harriet knocked on Leo's front door.

The four of them often walked to school together.

The door opened slowly, but no Leo appeared.

He was hiding behind the door.

"What's the matter, Leo?" asked Tabby.

"Can't you see?" said Leo's voice. "I've cut my hair!"

"No, we can't!" Tabby shouted. "We can't see through doors!"

"Leo," Connie said gently, "you can't stay home today.
Miss Roo is going to choose the actors for the
Robin Hood play. And you want to be Robin Hood so much!"

"Some Robin Hood I am," snapped Leo. "Looking like this,
I will never be Robin! You all go on without me."

Leo peered around the door to say goodbye to his friends.
But they weren't going anywhere.

"You can be Robin Hood," said Connie. "You can have
an imaginary bow and arrow and be the best archer
that ever lived. And you can pretend to have long hair,
if you like. After all, isn't that what acting is all about?"

"Easy for you to say," Leo told her sadly. "You've still got your hair."

"But I'm not the one who wants to be an actor," Connie pointed out.

Leo thought about this. Connie was right. A great actor could pretend to have long hair!

"Look," said Connie, "whenever you feel bad, just imagine yourself leading your friends through the forest. If you're a hero, nobody will care what your hair looks like."

Leo sighed. He picked up his school bag and came out from behind the door. "Let's go to school," he said.

When they got to school, Miss Roo remarked,
"Your hair looks very smart, Leo."

But Leo didn't say anything. His head felt
bare and small. "Is everybody looking at me?"
he whispered to Connie. "I feel funny with short hair."

"Hair or no hair, you are still you," Connie said.

Leo thought Connie didn't understand.

He remembered how he felt with long hair.

His hair made him feel big, strong and important.

Leo sat through the geography lesson with his head
hunched between his shoulders. All of a sudden,
he felt Connie prodding him.

"You are a great actor, remember!" she said.

Leo decided to listen to Connie's advice.

Leo sat up straight and pretended he was stretching his bow with an arrow. Zing! The arrow flew out and hit the bull's eye!

At playtime, Roddy and Tina were swinging from
the climbing frame when Leo came into the playground.

"Here comes Robin Hood the Hairless!" they teased.

Leo ignored them. He was still holding his imaginary
bow and arrow. And he was off to meet his friends
to practise for the play.

21

22

"There you are!" said Connie.

"Let's get ready," said Tabby. "I'll be Maid Marian. Connie can be Little John. Harriet can be the monk. And you, Leo, can be the young boy who grows up to be a hero and helps the poor."

"Let's all practise archery," said Leo.

"The old oak tree can be the forest," suggested Harriet.

They went over to the old oak tree and looked for
some branches and twigs. They made bows and arrows
with the branches and some bits of string.

"Now," said Tabby, "stand up tall
and straight. Ready, aim, fire!"

They all stretched their bows and let the twigs fly.

The twigs didn't fly very far, but everyone pretended they did.

Meanwhile, in the school hall, everyone else was busy preparing for the play. George was practising some scales on the piano.

Kit was painting thick green leaves on the stage wall
to make a forest. And Lisa and Martha were trying to
hang up a cardboard castle.

27

Miss Roo sat in the director's chair, below the stage.

Everyone wanted to play Robin Hood. Roddy was
the first to try. He came on stage riding his hobby horse.

"I'm Robin Hood," he cried. "I'm the greatest archer
in the world! There is no one better than me!"

But Roddy lost his balance and fell off the hobby horse. He was so angry he kicked it.

"Leo, you're on next," Miss Roo said with a smile.

Leo, Connie, Tabby and Harriet came on stage together.
They all looked great in their costumes. Leo was nervous,
but he started saying his lines.

Leo's voice rang out loud and clear, and soon all
his confidence came back.

"You are a great Robin Hood," said Miss Roo
as everyone clapped and cheered.

"Short hair must be good for your voice!" said Connie.

"Actually, I was thinking I might keep it this way,"
Leo said. "It might help me with my acting!"

Top of the Class
Collect them all!

Ellie Takes a Chance
Zuza Vrbova
Illustrated by Tom Morgan-Jones
1-84458-483-6

Zoë Wins the Race
Zuza Vrbova
Illustrated by Tom Morgan-Jones
1-84458-407-0

Piers Finds his Voice
Zuza Vrbova
Illustrated by Tom Morgan-Jones
1-84458-406-2

George Makes Friends
Zuza Vrbova
Illustrated by Tom Morgan-Jones
1-84458-482-8

Tabby Saves the Day
Zuza Vrbova
Illustrated by Tom Morgan-Jones
1-84458-481-X

Kit Paints the Sky
Zuza Vrbova
Illustrated by Tom Morgan-Jones
1-84458-404-6

Leo Takes to the Stage
Zuza Vrbova
Illustrated by Tom Morgan-Jones
1-84458-405-4

Roddy Learns a Lesson
Zuza Vrbova
Illustrated by Tom Morgan-Jones
1-84458-480-1

Visit the Top of the Class website at
www.topoftheclassbooks.com